Flick had run back around to the stall door, barking wildly. He stuck his muzzle through the bars until his nose touched one of Reflection's legs. Then he stood very still.

A soft growl started low in his throat, then got louder. He kept growling and snarling until it was quite loud. Then, between growls, he nipped Reflection's back legs. He continued to growl and bite over and over again.

At first no one noticed until Jack cried out. Everyone stopped talking and looked where Jack was pointing. "Look!" he yelled. "Look quick!"

FLICK THE HERO!

To Jenny —
One of my heroes...
an excellent reader!

I'm very proud of you!

Your friend —

(and Flick!)

L. Floyd Wyatt

.1997.

ALSO BY LYNN FLOYD WRIGHT

The Prison Bird
Just One Blade
Flick
Momma, Tell Me A Story

ALSO BY TONY WATERS

The Sailor's Bride
Just One Blade
Flick

FLICK THE HERO!

WRITTEN BY
LYNN FLOYD WRIGHT

ILLUSTRATED BY
TONY WATERS

WORRYWART PUBLISHING COMPANY

COLUMBIA

Worrywart Publishing Company
337 White Birch Circle
Columbia, South Carolina 29223-3228

Printed in the United States of America

1 3 5 7 9 10 8 6 4 2

Library of Congress Cataloging-in-Publication Data

Wright, Lynn Floyd, 1957 -
    Flick the hero! / written by Lynn Floyd Wright ; illustrated by
Tony Waters.
    p.   cm.
    Sequel to: Flick.
    Summary: Jack and his dog Flick are excited to be going for a week of fun at
his cousin Evan's horse farm, but their visit takes an unexpected turn for the
worse when Evan's horse Reflection falls dangerously ill.
    ISBN 1-881519-06-6 (hardcover :   alk. paper). -- ISBN 1-881519-07-4
(pbk.)
    (1. Horses--Fiction.   2. Dogs--Fiction.   3. Farm life--Fiction.
4. Cousins--Fiction.) I. Waters, Tony, 1958- ill.   II. Title.
PZ7. W9565Fn 1997
(Fic) --dc 21   96-45134
                                                             CIP
                                                             AC

To little Larry and Image, a real love story

LFW

To Charlene and Bubba, with love

TW

CHAPTER 1

Jack Coleman paced back and forth across the front porch of his house, pausing every few seconds to stick his head back through the front door. Flick followed right behind him.

"Come on, Dad. It's time to go. We should've left by now."

This had been the longest week of his life and he didn't think Friday would ever come. Today was the day he was going to his aunt and uncle's horse farm to spend a few days with his cousin Evan. And this time, he was going to a show and watch Evan and his horse, Reflection, compete.

But now Friday was finally here and it was time to go and his father was running late. 'Veterinarians have to eat too, like everybody else,' his mother would always say every time his father, Dr. Mike Coleman, jumped up in the middle of dinner to go tend to one of his sick "patients."

Jack started to call out again when he heard heavy footsteps on the stairs.

Flick barked and wagged his stumpy tail with delight

as Dr. Coleman stepped out into the late afternoon April sunlight. Both father and son were tall and thin with long, lanky legs and the same color dark red hair and green eyes.

"Let's get going you two," Dr. Coleman said as he stepped off the porch. "Unless you've changed your mind," he added with a wink.

Jack grabbed his duffel bag and started to follow. Flick jumped down the steps in one leap. Even after the accident, Jack was still amazed at all the things Flick could do with only two legs.

Jack shuddered every time he thought about it. Finding Flick on that cold morning, smashed down between the railroad ties, more dead than alive.

But looking at him now, it was almost impossible to believe that Flick had ever been hurt so badly. His silver and black coat gleamed in the sun and his two long legs practically bounced when he ran.

His father's voice broke into his thoughts. "Are you sure your aunt said Flick could come?" Dr. Coleman asked as Flick hopped up into the back seat of the white Jeep parked in the driveway.

"Sure, I'm sure," Jack answered, settling in the front seat. He watched as his father fiddled with something on the dashboard. *We'll never get there the way we're going,* Jack thought irritably.

Jack turned to grab his seat belt. Suddenly, his father snapped his fingers and climbed back out of the car. "Sorry, son," he said as he closed the door. "We can't go."

Jack looked at the closing door, his mouth wide open in disbelief.

CHAPTER 2

"Now, let me see," the elder Coleman said, walking back to open the hatch. "Did I get my medical bag? Your uncle wants me to check one of the horses while I'm there."

Jack blew his cheeks out in relief. "Dad, you've got it. I put it back there an hour ago. Let's just go, okay? It's going to be dark when we get there if we don't go now! And I might get to ride Reflection if we get there before dark."

"All right, just hold your horses," his father said, getting back into the Jeep. "Get it?" He poked Jack in the ribs. "Horses. Get it?"

Jack rolled his eyes, but couldn't help smiling. "Very funny. *Now* can we go?"

As the Jeep backed out of the drive, they both waved to Mrs. Coleman, who had stepped out on the porch to see them off.

Jack rolled down the window. The Jeep was quiet except for the whipping sound of warm air rushing through the open window. Jack leaned back against the headrest and looked out the window.

He was sure Reflection would win a ribbon at the show tomorrow. Out of all the horses his cousin Chris trained at the farm, Reflection was the coolest one of all. She was smart and really good-looking.

The Jeep passed the Lancaster, South Carolina town limits and headed south.

When it passed the Lancaster & Chester railroad station, Dr. Coleman suddenly hit the horn and tooted at Clifford Washington, the stationmaster. "Mr. Cliff," as everyone in town called him, waved back and broke into a huge grin when he heard Flick bark.

Flick had used his one front leg to prop himself up on the armrest. His head bobbed up and down out the window and his small tail vibrated with excitement. His schnauzer head, with its bushy eyebrows and floppy ears, blew back in the wind and his mouth hung open.

"Flick sure does love Cliff," Dr. Coleman noted. "Always has, ever since the first day you found him."

Jack nodded. "It's kinda weird, huh? I'm not sure I'd like someone who tried to shoot me."

They were both quiet when they thought about that

day. Jack still had nightmares reliving the scene.

Standing in the cold, looking first at Flick, then watching Mr. Cliff take aim with his pistol right at Flick's head. Then waiting for the sound of the shot...

A sudden sharp popping sound made Jack's head snap forward. A rock had hit the windshield. Jack relaxed his grip on his seat belt and leaned back again.

Then he realized his father was talking to him. "I'll tell you, I'd hate to think about not having Flick around. He's a pretty good old dog."

"No," Jack said solemnly as he reached back and grabbed Flick around the neck. "He's the best, smartest dog in the whole world." Flick curled his lips back, an expression that made him look like he was grinning. Then he licked Jack right in the ear!

Dr. Coleman chuckled. "I'm not so sure Alice thinks so. The last time he went with me to the farm, Flick was jumping around, barking and bossing the horses around like he owned the place!"

CHAPTER 3

The drive from Lancaster to Camden took half an hour. When they passed the Revolutionary War site of the Battle of Camden, Jack squirmed in his seat anxiously.

At the first road past the battlefield, a red and white wooden sign sat beside the road. A picture of a horse was at the top with the words BIT-A-BACK FARMS...PASO FINO HORSES and an arrow pointing to the left just below.

Dr. Coleman turned left off the highway, then went two more miles and turned right onto a dirt driveway.

The Jeep kicked up dust in its wake. Shading his eyes, Jack could barely see the farm in the distance at the end of the road.

Bit-A-Back Farms was exactly what its name implied, because it was set so far back from the road. It was made up of a large white wooden two-story house with a wrap-around porch and red shutters and a freshly painted red barn. Three fenced-in exercise corrals sat beside and behind the house and barn.

As Dr. Coleman and Jack pulled up next to the house, Alice Raney came out the screen door to greet them.

She flashed a smile at the car, then frowned a bit when she looked down at her watch.

"We were beginning to get worried," she said with re-lief, wiping her hands on the dish towel slung over her shoulder. "Evan's around back with the horses, Jack. You go on. Dinner's in about twenty minutes."

Jack waved goodbye to his father and headed in the direction of the stables. Flick leapt from the car and followed him.

CHAPTER 4

Jack called out to Evan as he reached the entrance to the barn. The strong smell of hay and manure greeted him at once. There were four stalls on his left, each occupied by paso fino horses of different colors and ages. The barn had twelve stalls in all.

Jack heard Evan call from around the corner. Flick flew past him and ran around to the other side of the barn, finding Evan first. Evan let out a surprised cry when Flick knocked him flat on his back.

"Hey, bud," Jack called as he reached them. "What's up?"

"Hey, yourself." Evan wasn't quite as tall as Jack was, but he was much bigger and heavier. His blond hair was buzz cut so that it looked more like a crew cut. He had his mother's blue eyes and a sly smile that always made people wonder what he was thinking. He wore his usual jeans and plaid flannel shirt and boots. But today he also wore a full length black plastic apron that covered him from neck to ankle.

"Where you been, man?" he asked once he had finally pulled Flick off of him. "We've been waiting for you." He had a brush in one hand and pointed inside the stall with his other one. A magnificent dapple gray mare with gentle brown eyes watched both boys from the back corner.

"Held up," Jack answered, looking inside the stall where Evan's finger had pointed. "You know my dad."

"Hey, Reflection," Jack said softly to the horse. Then to Evan, "she looks great. I still have time to ride her tonight, right?"

Evan wrinkled his brow. "Sorry. I asked Chris and he said no. Because of the show tomorrow. Trainers have their rules you know. Besides, I just fed her for the night."

Jack frowned and thought for a minute. Then his expression brightened. "But maybe he'll change his mind if I tell him I'll just walk her. Let's go ask him anyway. Come on."

Evan slid the stall door closed and the two boys started around the corner. "You coming, Flick?" Jack called over his shoulder. Flick stayed in front of the stall until the boys were gone. When they were out of sight, he paused and stuck his nose through the bars of the door.

He barked a couple of times, a pleasant rumbling sound that suggested a much bigger dog.

Reflection looked up from her food and walked over to where Flick was standing. Then she lowered her gray head and put it down next to the bars of the gate until her nose barely touched Flick's.

The two stood nose-to-nose for a minute or two. Then Flick dashed off with a delighted bark to find Jack and Evan.

CHAPTER 5

Jack and Evan found Chris in the corral behind the barn. He was riding a magnificent black stallion. Wilbur Raney, Chris and Evan's father, stood a few feet away holding a video camera. Neither greeted them when Jack and Evan walked up and stood on the fence.

"Watch this," Evan said to Jack in a whisper. "This is really cool."

Chris was walking the stallion over toward a four-foot wide floor of wooden boards that was set out in the middle of the corral. His right hand held the reins; in his left hand he balanced a silver tray with what looked to be a glass of wine on it.

He had on his best black riding outfit, a tuxedo with a short bolero jacket and round Spanish-style cowboy hat.

"What's he doing?" Jack quietly asked back. "I've never seen Chris do this before."

"Just keep watching," Evan said. "You'll see in a minute." As he spoke, Chris signaled to his father and instructed him to start taping. When the camera's red light came on, Chris nudged the horse with his thighs and moved him forward.

The horse stepped lively up onto the wooden flooring and pranced forward all the way to the end. Then he stopped, and at Chris' urging, began to walk backwards until he was back at the end he had started from.

Jack watched in awe at the horse's graceful movement and high prancing steps. The horse's hooves made a wonderful rhythmic tapping sound on the wood.

Horse and rider went backward and forward six times. Then they stopped. Wilbur Raney turned off the camera and walked over to Chris. "Okay. Got it. Nice job, Chris."

Chris nodded and handed the tray to his father. Then he led the horse down off the flooring and toward the barn.

Jack looked at Evan with a puzzled expression. "I still don't get it. What's the deal? Why does he use the tray?"

Evan smiled and jerked his head toward Chris and the horse. "It's like this. The reason people buy *Paso Fino* horses is because of their smooth style of moving. You know, *paso fino* even means "smooth step" in Spanish."

"But," Evan continued, "you know the horses still have to be trained and that's what Chris does."

"Yeah, I know all that," Jack said impatiently.

"Well," Evan said cutting him off, "what Chris was doing was making a video to show the horse's owners. Did you notice how none of the wine spilled out of the glass?"

Jack nodded as he watched Chris and the stallion disappear into the barn.

"Chris was holding that tray," Evan continued, "to show exactly how smoothly the horse has learned to move. That horse can now prance so smoothly that Chris can even carry a glass of wine and not spill a drop. That's the sign of a healthy, well-trained *paso fino*. Cool, huh?"

Jack agreed. Suddenly Alice Raney's voice sounded from the direction of the house. "Dinner's on the table. Let's eat."

CHAPTER 6

Jack groaned with pleasure. He ate too much at dinner and now he was sleepy.

He was lying on the floor in the den with Flick asleep on his chest. A full stomach and Flick's warm body moving up and down in rhythm with his own made his eyelids heavy. To keep from dozing off, he stared at the ceiling.

He was really looking forward to tomorrow. Evan and Reflection were going to wipe out all those other horses. And he'd be there to see it.

"Let's go out and say goodnight to Reflection." Evan's voice broke the silence. The two got up off the floor and headed out into the yard.

Flick ran ahead of them and grabbed a stick from the ground and started throwing it to himself in the air.

Evan laughed. "One funny dog you got there, man. I wish I had one like him."

The barn was filled with the nightly sounds of soft whinnies and muted snorts from the horses getting ready for sleep.

When they got to Reflection's stall, Evan checked the straw bedding. Then he refilled Reflection's water bucket.

Jack watched as he then went to a sack and scooped out a small handful of grain.

Reflection neighed and ate the treat right from Evan's hand. While she chewed, Evan leaned next to her and put his face close. He talked softly to her for a minute.

"We're gonna nail those other guys tomorrow, Reflection," he murmured, massaging her on the nose. "You and me. They'll eat our dust."

Chris came from around the corner. "I'm ready to call it a night, guys," he said to Jack and Evan. "You too, Flick." He patted Flick's head. "Tomorrow's a big day."

CHAPTER 7

Groaning, Chris sat up in his bed and stretched. He looked at the clock on his bedside table. Twelve-thirty. "I'm going to kill that horse," he grumbled.

He knew exactly who was making that awful racket. Lightning, the latest arrival to the farm, was playing with his water bucket again. The horse thought it was a fun game to play and had been doing it every day for the two weeks he had been at Bit-A-Back. This was the third time today.

Pulling on his jeans and boots, Chris made his way from his room down the darkened stairs and into the den. The rest of the house was asleep. He grabbed a flashlight and started out for the barn.

The sound was getting louder. "It's a wonder anybody can sleep," he said as he stepped out the back door.

Chris quickly walked into the barn and rounded the corner to Lightning's stall. The thrashing sound was incredibly loud. Chris directed the flashlight inside.

To his amazement Lightning was standing quietly in a back corner staring back at him. His water bucket stood in the opposite corner, upright and untouched.

Still the noise continued. But it was so close it could only be coming from the stall next door. Stall number six.

It wouldn't be...? Chris thought, then moved in that direction.

His jaw dropped and his eyes grew wide with horror when he looked inside.

CHAPTER 8

Reflection was on her side moaning. Chris moved swiftly to the stall door and unlocked it. Grabbing the door handle, he pulled on it. It didn't budge.

Switching the flashlight from his hand to under his chin, he grabbed the handle again, this time with both hands and tugged as hard as he could. The door remained closed tight.

Chris repositioned the flashlight back in his hand and looked inside the stall again.

Reflection continued to groan. Sweat covered her dappled body and her stomach was bloated. Chris called to her.

"Reflection, look here girl." He tried to keep his voice calm. "Look at me. Look here!"

The horse's eyes were glazed and rolled back into her head. Her moaning got louder.

Chris saw then why the stall door wouldn't open. In her pain, Reflection had managed to get her body wedged between the door and the adjacent wall with her back feet tangled in the bars.

All his years of experience with horses told Chris that as long as Reflection stayed in that position, the door would stay jammed. He'd have to go in another way.

Leaving the stall door unlocked, he ran quickly around to the side of the stall where a small window sat about six feet off of the ground. Chris threw open the shutters and went looking for a stool or a step ladder.

"Chris, what's the matter?" Alice Raney called from the entrance of the barn. She had on her bathrobe and tennis shoes. Her face looked pale in the dim light. "What is it, son?" she asked again, searching his face. "Is it Amorosa? Is she foaling?"

"Momma, Reflection's real sick," Chris answered her, still looking frantically for the stool. "Call Uncle Mike! Quick!"

"What's wrong with her?" she asked. But one look at Chris' face told her that this wasn't the time to ask questions. Without another word, she turned and hurried back towards the house.

CHAPTER 9

Chris found the step ladder behind some sacks of oats and went back to the window. He hoisted himself up and tried the opening. It was too small for him. He got only his head and shoulders through before he was stuck.

Inside, Reflection was still groaning. She was sweating even heavier and her breathing was much harder than before. Her sides heaved and her breath came in ragged bursts.

Chris tried going through again, this time sideways. Still he got stuck halfway through. On the third try, he heard voices coming toward him.

Wilbur and Alice Raney, Jack and Evan were all talking at once. Flick was barking and running back and forth from the stall door to the window.

"Mike's on his way," Wilbur said when Chris struggled back through the window to join them. "Now, what can I do to help you?"

They could all hear Reflection's moans. "Dad, we've got to find a way to get in there. I'm too big. We've got to get Reflection up and walking before..."

His voice trailed off when he looked at his little brother. Evan looked like he was about to cry. Then his expression changed and he looked mad. "I'll go! Let me go!"

Chris looked sadly at him. "If I can't get through there, no way you can, Evan. You're even broader than I am." Then he looked at his father. "Dad, here's what I'm thinking. We can pull the bars off of the front with the truck and a chain. I can't think of anything else."

"Let me try," Jack said, interrupting them. He stepped forward. "I might be skinny enough to get through."

"Worth a try," Wilbur said to Chris. "If not, we can always try with the truck. Come on, Jack, up you go."

The two men lifted Jack feet first up to the window. When he had gotten through as far as his hips, Jack put his arms on each side of the window and pushed himself through. Outside, Flick was jumping up and down, trying to follow.

Jack fell into the stall and landed softly on the hay. "Okay, Jack," Chris instructed, "take this and put it around Reflection's neck." He handed Jack a halter and lead rope.

Jack strode quickly over beside the horse and gasped. Lather covered Reflection's body and mouth, and her gums were starting to turn blue.

Fighting back the sour taste in his mouth, Jack gently lifted the horse's head and slipped the halter around her neck.

"All right, Jack. Good job," Chris said. "Now bring the rope to me."

Jack did as he was told. Flick kept barking and running back and forth. "Flick, shut up !" Evan yelled and kicked at him. "Jack, make him shut up!"

CHAPTER 10

"Hey!" Jack shot back, trying to climb back through the window. "He's just worried too. You kick at him again and I'll cream you!"

"Both of you. Quiet. Now!!" Alice Raney's voice silenced them both. Ignoring them, Chris was tugging on the rope and talking to the downed horse. "Come on, baby," he coaxed. "On your feet, girl. You can do it. Come on," he said again in a soothing voice.

Jack was trying to help him pull but Reflection just wouldn't budge. Chris noticed with growing dread that now the horse's eyes were completely rolled back into her head.

"Come on, Reflection." The panic in Chris' voice was starting to show. He tugged harder on the rope.

Flick had run back around to the stall door, barking wildly. He stuck his muzzle through the bars until his nose touched one of Reflection's legs. Then he stood very still.

A soft growl started low in his throat, then got louder. He kept growling and snarling until it was quite loud. Then, between growls, he nipped Reflection's back legs.

FLICK THE HERO!

He kept growling and biting over and over again.

   At first no one noticed until Jack cried out. Everyone stopped talking and looked where Jack was pointing. "Look!" he yelled. "Look quick!"

CHAPTER 11

As they watched, Reflection's head moved slightly and her eyes came back into view. She gave a weak whinny.

Jack dropped his part of the rope and ran over to the window. "Come here, Flick," he commanded. When Flick came, he told Chris, "hand him up to me."

Jack set him down softly beside him. Flick ran quickly to Reflection's side, his two legs throwing out hay in all directions.

"Worth a try, Jack," Chris said as Evan, Wilbur and Alice crowded in around behind him to see what was happening. "All right, here we go again. Flick, get her up!"

Flick stood directly above Reflection's head and poked her muzzle with his own. Then, moving to his right, he began snapping at the horse's front legs, moving quickly back out of the way when they twitched.

While Flick was busy, Chris and Jack kept tugging on the rope. The first three times they pulled, nothing happened. But Reflection was getting more agitated with every bite of Flick's sharp little teeth.

"Keep it up, Flick!" Jack cried. His arms and legs ached from the constant pulling and prodding.

The next time Flick's teeth sunk into one of Reflection's legs, the horse raised her head and shoulders a little off the ground. She groaned again.

"Don't let loose, Jack," Chris ordered. "Now, give it all you've got." They both pulled with all their strength.

Just as Reflection was about to fall back down, Flick took one final swipe at her legs. The horse snorted, blowing foam from her mouth and nostrils, and stood up!

"Okay, Jack, keep hold of your end." Jack rocked back on his heels, keeping the rope taut. "That's good," Chris said. "Now walk closer to her and hold her steady." Chris handed his end of the rope to his father.

Jack kept walking closer to Reflection, talking to her in soothing tones. By the time he had moved close enough to get a grip on the halter, Chris was at the stall door.

Flinging the door open so hard it rattled on its track, Chris strode over and grabbed the rope from Jack.

CHAPTER 12

"Dad, you can let go of your end," Chris instructed. "I've got her." He held tightly to the halter and patted Reflection on the nose.

"Let's get her out into the yard." Evan had brought a fresh blanket from the barn and fastened it loosely around Reflection's body. Very slowly Chris, aided by Wilbur, led the horse out of the stall into the field behind the barn. Reflection followed very slowly on shaky legs.

While Alice went inside to make coffee, Jack, Evan and Flick followed the two men at a distance. They watched in silence as Chris walked Reflection back and forth across the width of the field. Twice the horse tried to stop, but Chris tightened his hold on the rope and kept her moving.

They had just walked the field once when Mike Coleman pulled into the driveway.

Dr. Coleman walked briskly toward the group assembled in the field. Flick ran up to meet him, barking excitedly.

"How is she?" he asked without wasting any time on small talk. His eyes narrowed with concern at the sight.

He walked along with Chris and Reflection to make sure that the horse kept moving. "I've practically had to pull her along," Chris said. "She's really shaky. I don't think she can stay on her feet much longer."

"Bring her over here," Dr. Coleman said, pointing to a pile of hay. Chris did as he was instructed. Dr. Coleman unfastened the blanket and let it drop to the ground.

"Now just hold her up until I say to let go," the vet said. He reached into his medical bag, extracted a needle and small bottle of liquid and gave Reflection a tranquilizer.

The horse barely twitched when the needle was inserted. "This'll help slow her pulse down," Dr. Coleman said as he gently pulled the syringe out. "Okay, we can let her lie down now."

While he was working, Evan, Jack and Flick stood back in the shadows, watching. Evan chewed nervously on his lower lip. The muscles in his jaw clenched and unclenched. Jack put an arm around him and Flick licked his hand.

"It'll be okay," Jack said to him in a low voice. "You know my dad's the best. She'll be all right. You'll see."

Evan nodded but didn't say anything. He swallowed hard and Jack could tell he was trying hard not to cry.

Flick kept licking Evan's hand, then stopped suddenly and ran off.

The two boys watched as Flick ran to where Chris, Dr. Coleman, and Wilbur were standing with Reflection.

Dr. Coleman was pulling his stethoscope from his ears. "There's no gut sounds coming from her stomach at all. A blockage for sure."

"Colic. I knew it," Chris slapped his thigh in disgust and spit the words out. It was one of the worst things any horse owner could hear.

Mike Coleman nodded grimly. "Afraid so. Reflection's going to have to have surgery. And soon. I'll go make some calls. Georgia is about the closest place I can think of. One of my old classmates, Dr. Walker Braxton, is a surgeon there at the University of Georgia. He's worked on lots of horses like Reflection."

Wilbur nodded. "Let's go inside and see if you can reach him."

FLICK THE HERO!

While they were talking, Flick nudged at Reflection but got no response. She lay calmer now that the tranquilizer had gone to work, but was still sweating heavily.

Flick tried prodding her again, then stopped and lay down and curled up beside the horse's head.

CHAPTER 13

"Everything's all set, Wilbur." Mike Coleman hung up the phone and looked at his brother-in-law. "You and I had better get going. They're expecting Reflection in a few hours."

Everyone except Chris and Flick had moved from the yard into the kitchen. Wilbur sighed heavily as Alice handed him a cup of coffee.

"I'll go give Chris and you a hand loading her up," he said as he stood up and headed toward the screen door.

The two men were almost at the door when the voice from behind stopped them. "I'm going." Evan had been sitting on one of the kitchen stools, listening.

The room fell silent. Everyone turned to look at Evan. "I don't think that's a good idea." Wilbur stepped around Dr. Coleman and walked back to where Evan was sitting with Jack. "It's going to be a long ride, son, and things might be rough. I just don't think you should go. Because if..."

Before he could finish, Alice finished his sentence. "Could I see you in the den a minute, dear?" Wilbur started to protest then shrugged, turned and followed her.

"I'll be outside," Mike Coleman said, looking at Jack and jerking his head toward the door. "Anybody else want to give me a hand?"

Jack jabbed Evan's shoulder with his fist and turned to follow his father. Evan started to get up, then changed his mind and slumped back down on his stool.

When they got outside, Jack and Dr. Coleman helped Chris fill the floor of the horse trailer with clean cedar shavings. They took the center divider out to make enough room for Reflection to lie down.

Jack stood nearby holding Flick while the two men pulled Reflection back to her feet and led her into the trailer. Just as she got inside and lay down, Wilbur, Alice and Evan came out of the house.

Without saying a word, Evan climbed into the back and sat down by his horse. He took the fresh blanket he had brought from the house and laid it over Reflection. Then he pressed his head down on his horse's body.

"Let's go," Wilbur said. He turned to Chris. "I know you'll do well tomorrow. Sorry I won't be there to watch. But you know I'll be thinking of you."

FLICK THE HERO!

Mike Coleman looked at Jack and Flick. "Son, I've already called your mother. But you call her when you get up so she won't be worried. I know you'll be good and mind your aunt."

Jack nodded and moved out of the way. He held on to Flick very tightly as he watched the pickup and trailer head out into the night.

CHAPTER 14

"Everyone back in the house. No use standing out here all night. We need to try and get some rest." Alice put her arm around Jack and Flick and steered them back toward the screen door.

Chris turned back to go into the barn to check on the other horses. "Be right in," he called.

Inside in the kitchen, Alice poured Jack a steaming cup of hot chocolate. "This will help you sleep." She looked up at the clock, which told her it was two-fifteen. "Although," she added, "we'll be getting back up soon enough. Got to leave by seven."

Chris entered the house, yawning and stretching, then started for the stairs. "I think I'm too keyed up to sleep, but I'm going to try anyway. Make sure I'm up by five, okay?"

Alice nodded, then pointed Jack in the same direction. Flick was already halfway up the steps. Jack suddenly felt so tired. His feet felt so heavy that walking seemed too great an effort to make. He trudged up to the top and looked back down at his aunt. She looked as tired as he felt.

"I'll be up to check on you in a minute. Get on into bed." Jack gave her a weak smile and went to his room.

As he lay in bed, even as tired as he was, he couldn't go to sleep. His mind kept buzzing with all kinds of questions. *Where were they now? Was Reflection going to be okay?*

He looked at Flick sleeping peacefully at his feet. *Poor Evan. I know how I'd feel if it was Flick that was hurt.*

He closed his eyes and tried not to think. After a long while, the soothing sound of Flick's soft snoring made him relax. He said a quick prayer and soon his dog's familiar gentle wheezing was the last thing he heard as he finally drifted off to sleep.

CHAPTER 15

A gentle, persistent shaking made Jack open his eyes. Flick was jumping up and down on the bed, making it jiggle. "All right, all right. I'm up!" he said a little crossly. But Flick just kept bouncing up and down, trying to lick him in the face.

Jack laughed. "You are one weird dog, you know that?" he said to Flick. "But I'm keeping you anyway." Jack rolled over on his side and picked up his watch. "Six o' clock! Why'd you let me sleep so late?"

He hustled downstairs to find his aunt in the kitchen. She smiled at the sight of him, his hair sticking out in all directions, his pajama bottoms all rumpled up.

"Why'd you let me sleep so late?" he asked again. "We're still going to the show right?" Then he caught himself. "I mean, did my dad call? How's Reflection? She's going to be all right, isn't she?"

Alice held up her hands. "Whoa, boy!" she said. "One thing at a time." She sat down heavily on one of the kitchen stools. When Jack sat down beside her she started to explain. "First of all, your dad *did* call. The surgery just finished about a half hour ago." Her mouth drew into a tight line. She paused, choosing her words.

"Reflection is holding her own, Jack. That's about the best that can be said right now. She survived the surgery. I won't go into all the details. They're rather gory. Reflection did have colic. That's like a real bad stomach ache in horses. It messes up their insides."

"And Reflection had a very, very bad case, your dad said. But the doctors took care of it. Now, we just have to wait and see."

Jack started to ask something but his aunt continued. "The next few hours are critical. If Reflection can make it through them, then we worry about the next few days. If she gets past the first week, things will really start looking good."

"How's Evan?" Jack managed to squeak out. He could see that Alice's eyes were starting to fill up with tears.

"He's upset, but he's all right. He's staying close to Reflection. He and your uncle and your dad are going to stay there today and come home tomorrow."

She stood up suddenly and brushed at her eyes. "Enough of that." Then as if she could read his mind, "we've still got a show to get to. Go get dressed. We've got to get on the road."

CHAPTER 16

As the truck and trailer rolled through the night on the way back from the show in Asheville, Jack closed his eyes and let his mind wander.

He pretended to be asleep so no one would bother him. So he kept his eyes tightly squeezed shut and listened to the conversation going on beside him between Chris and one of the hired hands from Bit-A-Back.

The ride to Asheville yesterday morning had been long. Now it seemed even longer coming back from that stupid show. The show. What he had been looking forward to for weeks. Now it had come and gone and it wasn't even any fun.

First of all, Flick had to stay back at the farm because dogs weren't allowed at the shows. What a stupid rule!

Then his aunt had decided to stay behind in case his dad called with news about Reflection.

Reflection. Poor Reflection and Evan. Stuck in Georgia. Who knew what was happening there now?

Flick and Evan and Reflection. Without them for company he had been lonely wandering around the show grounds all by himself.

Except for Chris winning a couple of first place blue ribbons, the rest of the show had been a two-day blur of horses and riders of all sizes and ages.

But when it was time for the event Evan and Reflection were supposed to be riding in, he had gotten depressed again. He'd watched the other kids in Evan's class line up and prance around the ring. His spirits sank.

"Those other guys couldn't touch Evan and Reflection. It's just not fair," he said softly under his breath.

He got so mad thinking about the whole thing that he almost didn't notice that the truck had pulled to a stop. He heard a door open and felt somone gently shake his shoulder.

"We're home, Jack," Chris said softly.

Jack opened his eyes and glared at him. "*Your* home maybe," he said under his breath. "But tomorrow Flick and I are going to *our* home. And we won't be coming back here. Ever."

CHAPTER 17

The phone call came a week after Jack and Flick got home from Bit-A-Back Farms.

Jack, with Flick tagging alongside, had just barged through the back door holding up a string of bass he had caught. "Hey, Mom!" he yelled, walking from room to room. "Where are you? Look what Flick and I got!"

"She's not here," Dr. Coleman said, covering his hand over the receiver of the phone and signaling for him to be quiet. Then he spoke back into the phone. "Hold on Evan. He just came in. I'll get him."

Jack tried to casually back out of the room, hoping that he could slip out without being noticed. When he got almost to the doorway, his father's voice stopped him cold. "Here. It's for you." He thrust the phone at Jack.

"I've got Evan on the phone," he said. "And you're *going* to talk to him." Jack shook his head and looked at his father pleadingly.

"Dad, please..." he started. Dr. Coleman kept his hand over the receiver and stepped right into Jack's face. "He's your cousin and he's been very upset about his horse."

"You didn't say two decent words to him before we left last week. That mumbling you did was hardly an apology. Now you're going to talk to him and you're going to do it now. Do you understand me?"

Jack swallowed hard and nodded. When his father talked like that, he knew he was stuck. Jack handed him the fish and took the phone.

"Hey," he said a little uncertainly. The voice on the other end of the phone was equally ill at ease.

"Hey, yourself," Evan said back. "How's it going?"

"Okay," Jack answered. He paused, too embarrassed to mention Reflection's name. Instead he asked, "how's everybody?"

The sudden sharpness in Evan's voice shocked him. "How do you think everybody is, Jack?" he cried, raising his voice. "You mean how is Reflection? Well, she isn't good. She isn't good at all. The vets in Georgia say she's depressed. She won't eat. Doesn't even like to walk around the paddock like she used to."

"We're bringing her home tomorrow for all the good it'll do," he continued without taking a breath.

"I don't think she cares if she comes home or not. But it sure was nice of you to ask," he added sarcastically.

Jack jerked the phone away and looked at his father helplessly. Dr. Coleman's look made him put it back up to his ear. "Well, I, uh, what I mean is," he sputtered. He felt like a real rat. He couldn't think of anything to say. "Uh, Evan, I'm really sorry..."

A sobbing sound drowned out his words. Jack listened, embarrassed. When they stopped after a minute, Evan managed to speak.

"Even I can't make her feel better. Dad's taken me to see her twice already and it doesn't seem to make any difference. I just don't think she cares." Evan sniffed and cleared his throat a few times, then started to mumble a goodbye.

"Well, sorry to bother you," he said, getting that edgy tone in his voice again. "See you around maybe."

"Wait!" Jack blurted out before Evan could hang up. "How about if Flick and I went with you to get her? Couldn't hurt. I mean it might help. You wouldn't mind, would you? But we won't come if you really don't want us to."

Evan's tone changed immediately. "That would be great. I'll tell Dad. We're leaving at nine. See you tomorrow!"

He hung up, leaving Jack holding the phone and listening to dead air.

CHAPTER 18

"That was a good thing you did," Dr. Coleman said to Jack as the Jeep rambled down the road the next morning towards the Bit-A-Back. "I'm proud of you, son."

Jack didn't answer. He just kept staring out the window. *I'm such a jerk,* he thought. *Evan wouldn't have treated me this way if something bad had happened to Flick.*

Flick was going back to the farm with them. He was in the back seat again, but on this trip, even he was quiet. Instead of his usual bouncing up and down out of the window, he lay in a tight ball on the seat, his two legs curled under his body. He lay perfectly still, but he wasn't asleep. His eyes, normally so bright, stared sadly straight ahead.

But when Dr. Coleman turned onto the dirt road leading to the farm, Flick suddenly started barking and his whole body shook with anticipation. Even Jack had to laugh in spite of his uneasiness.

"I swear he knows he's going to the farm," he told his father, looking back at Flick. "How can he possibly know?"

Dr. Coleman reached back to pat Flick's head. "How does Flick do any of the things he does? He walks, he jumps fences just like a normal dog, he even carries your fishing rod in his mouth without falling over. I can't explain it, even though I'm a veterinarian. He's just a miracle."

****

The ride to Georgia was equally quiet. Neither Jack nor Evan had much to say, so they mostly listened to their fathers. Wilbur was filling Dr. Coleman in on the latest arrivals at Bit-A-Back.

When they turned into the stable area behind the University of Georgia Veterinary School of Medicine, Wilbur parked the truck and trailer.

As soon as they stopped, Flick began jumping up and down on the seat beside Jack. When Evan started to open the back door, Flick crouched down low, ready to leap out.

Before he could scamper down, Dr. Coleman grabbed him by the collar. "No, Flick," he said, holding him down. "You stay in here until I find out if it's okay for you to be running around loose."

Flick whimpered and crouched back down in the seat. He stuck his nose through the crack in the window and started to cry. When everyone had gotten out of the car, Jack pointed to the pasture directly in front of them.

A short distance away, a young man in a green smock was leading a gray dappled horse on a rope. "Look! There she is! It's Reflection!" Jack cried. "Come on, Evan. Let's..."

Suddenly Jack bit off his words and looked again at the scene in front of him. Something was definitely wrong. Reflection was barely moving.

Actually, Jack observed, it seemed that the man was almost having to pull her along. What's more, Reflection's head was hanging very low to the ground.

"I tried to tell you," Evan said, moving alongside Jack. "They say she's depressed. Can you believe it? Just wait 'til we get closer. She won't even lift her head up when she sees me."

"Maybe she will today," Jack answered, trying to sound convincing. "Maybe she's feeling better today, you know?" But Evan only shook his head again and again.

When they reached the field, while Dr. Coleman and Wilbur walked over to talk to the attendant, Jack and Evan went to see Reflection.

As Evan had said, the horse didn't even look up.

CHAPTER 19

"Hey, Reflection," Evan said, rubbing the side of his horse's head and muzzle. "How you doing, girl? Glad to see me?" But Reflection just stood there, with her head hanging down.

Jack noticed that Reflection was a lot skinnier than he'd ever seen her. Plus, she had an angry-looking red line from the stitches that were running the length of her belly underneath.

Jack reached into his pocket and pulled out an apple that he'd brought with him. He placed it in the middle of his hand and offered it to the horse.

"Reflection, look what I brought you, girl! Here you go!" Jack said, thrusting the apple down so the horse could see it.

Reflection watched with dull eyes as the apple thudded to the ground when Jack let go.

"What's the use?" Evan turned away and started back toward the truck, hands buried deep in the pockets of his jeans. In the distance, Jack could still hear Flick whining and barking like crazy.

What can I do? Think! Jack told himself.

He turned to follow his cousin. When he looked up ahead, he saw that Evan had already reached the truck. Before Jack could warn him, Evan angrily yanked the door open and Flick hit the ground running!

"Grab him!" he yelled to Evan. But it was too late. Evan was too slow and in a second's time, Flick was past him and heading right for Jack!

CHAPTER 20

"I'll get him!" Jack got down in a crouch, hands out in front ready to move suddenly in any direction to catch his dog.

Flick started right for him, then at the last minute swerved to the left. Jack lunged at him and fell flat on his face in the dirt.

"Jack, catch your dog! Flick, you stop right there!" Dr. Coleman had stopped talking with the attendant and was running after Flick.

Flick stopped dead in his tracks. "Flick, you stay right there!" Dr. Coleman repeated as he got closer.

Flick cocked his head and grinned at him. Just as Dr. Coleman got ready to grab him by the collar, Flick suddenly took off again!

By now everyone, including the attendant, was watching Flick. While Jack and his father chased him unsuccessfully, Flick ran straight to the field where Reflection was standing.

Flick stopped right in front of Reflection and barked once. Reflection pricked up her ears and looked up for a few seconds. Then her head drooped again.

Flick slowly began to circle the horse over and over again, sniffing her and nudging at her legs. After five passes, Flick walked very slowly up to Reflection's face and stopped. He nuzzled Reflection on the nose and then lay down at her feet.

Reflection watched with curiosity. She looked at Flick for a moment or two, then nudged Flick's body with her head.

Jack and Dr. Coleman had reached the gate to the field. But before Jack could call out, Dr. Coleman put a hand on his shoulder, telling him to wait.

At that moment, Flick did something Jack had never seen him do before. Flick leaned up and licked Reflection right on the nose.

Reflection picked up her head and looked around. With everyone watching in disbelief, she snorted a few times, and after a minute or two, took off in a slow walk across the field!

Flick woofed happily and chased off after her.

EPILOGUE

Jack and Dr. Coleman stood perched on the wooden fence surrounding the show ring and watched the riders. Flick sat below them, his little tail flicking from side to side at the sight of all the people and horses. He barked from time to time, but didn't run off.

The last Saturday event of the day at the National Paso Fino Horse Championships in Atlanta was taking place in the ring. Chris had already ridden in all his events and had gone back to the stables to care for his horses.

"I still can't figure out why Chris wanted me to come," Jack said to his father. "I've already seen him ride at the show in Asheville. And why did he say it was okay for Flick to come? He didn't get to come last time."

Dr. Coleman squinted in the waning August sunlight and shrugged his shoulders. "I really don't know. Anyway, it was good for me to see Chris ride in national competition. I'm glad we could be here to see it. But we'd better get going. School starts on Monday."

Jack groaned as he jumped down from the fence. "Don't remind me. The summer went too fast."

Dr. Coleman smiled. "It always does, son. Let's stop

by the stables and say goodbye."

As they pushed through the crowd still gathered around the ring, the sudden crackle of the loudspeaker made them stop.

"Ladies and gentlemen, may I have your attention please? Would Jack and Flick Coleman please report to the judges' table ringside immediately? Jack and Flick Coleman, report to the judges' table ringside immediately."

Jack wrinkled his brow and looked at his father. "What do they want us for? Flick didn't do anything wrong. Didn't Chris say it was okay for him to come?"

Dr. Coleman looked equally puzzled. "Only one way to find out. Let's go."

When they reached the side entrance to the ring. Dr. Coleman stepped forward. "Wait here. I'll go see what's going on."

Jack held onto Flick and waited nervously while his father walked through the gate and began talking to a lady seated at a large table. Jack couldn't hear what they were saying but he noticed that mostly the lady was talking and his father was listening. At first his father was smiling, but after a few minutes he began to frown.

As Jack watched, the ring was cleared of all riders and their horses. When they left, a man carrying a small barrel about four feet high came into the center of the ring. He put it down near the end of the wooden planking the horses had been walking on and left.

After a few minutes, Dr. Coleman motioned to Jack and Flick.

"Man, what did we do?" Jack asked Flick. He held onto him a little tighter and walked to where his father and the lady were standing.

"Jack," the lady said, "you and Flick follow me please." Jack stared at his father as if he'd lost his mind, but his father looked him straight in the eye. "Go on," he said a bit sternly.

"But what did...?" Jack stammered. "Just follow me please," the lady repeated. "I'll be right here when you get back," his father added. "Go ahead."

Jack narrowed his eyes at his father. "Fine," he said.

"Come on, Flick."

Flick lay very stiffly in Jack's arms as the two turned to follow the lady. As they walked to the center of the ring, Jack noticed that everyone seemed to be staring at them.

The loudspeaker came to life again. "Ladies and gentlemen, your attention please. We have a very special event scheduled that is not listed in your program. Please direct your attention to the center of the ring."

The lady stopped in front of the barrel and turned around to face Jack. "Please place your dog up here," she said, patting the barrel. "And hold him tightly so he doesn't jump down."

Beads of sweat had popped out on Jack's face. Flick was still rigid in his arms and the silver hair on the back of his neck bristled.

The crowd buzzed anxiously. Everyone was looking at the boy and dog stranded in the center of the ring. Jack felt his face get hot.

The lady didn't smile. She just kept looking at Jack in a curious way and patting the barrel.

"Wait here," she said and left. Jack stood there, staring at his feet, wishing the ground would open and swallow Flick and him up.

Suddenly the corral gate opened. A hush fell over the crowd. Jack looked up and couldn't believe his eyes. He was stunned. Too stunned to speak. Flick stood up, his stumpy tail thumping wildly on the barrel.

Coming toward the two was Evan. And he was riding Reflection! Reflection walked proudly, head held high, gray body lean and strong. The muscles in her sides rippled when she moved and her tail and mane glistened in the late Saturday sun. Evan had on his show outfit, a tuxedo and round black felt Spanish riding hat. His right hand held the reins; in his left he balanced a silver tray with a wine glass on top.

Jack started to run toward them, but Evan held up his hand and motioned for them to stay where they were. Jack put his hand down on Flick's back to restrain him.

"Ladies and gentlemen, your attention please," the voice on the speaker started again. "Please watch the center ring."

At that moment, urging his horse on, Evan guided Reflection onto the wooden planking in the ring. Reflection moved smoothly and effortlessly, with no sign of her injury four months ago.

Evan led his horse forward and backward over the planking, tray in hand. It was just like Chris had done with the black stallion that day at the farm!

The crowd held its breath as the boy and horse went through their routine. After Evan and Reflection had gone up and back the boards three times, they stopped. Not a drop had spilled out of the glass!

Then the loudspeaker roared once more. "Ladies and gentlemen, your attention again please. Many of you know the horse and rider in the ring. Many of you have competed against Evan Raney and his horse Reflection. And many of you know that Reflection was gravely ill and almost died a few months back."

Not a sound could be heard from the spectators.

"But what you may not know," the voice continued, "is that the young man standing in the center of the ring is Evan Raney's cousin Jack Coleman. And that young Jack's dog, Flick, saved Reflection's life."

A loud "oh" went up from the crowd. "Therefore in honor of his special act of heroism and compassion," the loudspeaker continued, "we at the National Paso Fino Horse Association are proud to give a special honorary show award to Flick Coleman."

Evan leaned down and handed the tray and glass to the attendant who had reentered the ring. He reached into the pocket of his jacket and put something around his neck. Then he and Reflection trotted towards Jack and Flick. Something shiny hit Jack's eyes, blinding him. He shaded his eyes with his hand to get a better look.

It wasn't until Evan had gotten down from his horse that Jack could see what the shiny object was that had blinded him. It was a gold medallion with the inscription NPFHA HERO at the top and the name FLICK COLEMAN at the bottom.

Evan took it off and placed it around Flick's neck. He put one arm around Flick's body and stroked his head. "Thanks, Flick," he whispered. "I owe you a big one, boy."

Then he broke into a huge grin and grabbed Jack in a headlock. "You too," he said, his voice breaking just a bit. "Gotcha, didn't I? Can I keep a surprise or what?"

Jack couldn't think of anything to say. He looked back at his father who was grinning from ear to ear. Jack smiled back and then released his hold on Flick.

Flick broke loose from his grasp and leapt down off the barrel and went to stand beside Reflection. The two then began running, side by side, around the inside of the ring.

The crowd roared.

ABOUT THE AUTHOR

LYNN FLOYD WRIGHT is crazy about animals! And in *Flick the Hero!*, her fifth book for children, she has picked two of her most favorite subjects-- dogs and horses-- to create a story that will again delight animal lovers everywhere. Although her other books for children, *The Prison Bird, Just One Blade, Flick* and *Momma, Tell Me A Story,* have each enjoyed worldwide acclaim, the *Flick* books remain her favorite to write and read aloud to her family. She and her husband Dave have four children and share their house in Columbia, South Carolina with two dogs -- a schnauzer/ poodle mix named Skipper (the model for Flick) and a miniature schnauzer named Nellie.

ABOUT THE ILLUSTRATOR

TONY WATERS has been drawing since he was old enough to hold a crayon. His first book, *The Sailor's Bride,* which he wrote and illustrated, was published in March of 1991. A graduate of Furman University in Greenville, South Carolina, he currently works with an architectural firm in Charleston and lives with his two cats on John's Island, South Carolina. This is his third collaborative effort with Lynn Floyd Wright.

ORDER OTHER BOOKS BY LYNN FLOYD WRIGHT

QUANTITY	TITLE	PRICE	TOTAL
_____	**THE PRISON BIRD** (hardback only)	**$12.95**	_____
_____	**JUST ONE BLADE** (hardback only)	**$12.95**	_____
_____	**FLICK** (hardback)	**$12.95**	_____
_____	**FLICK** (paperback)	**$ 7.95**	_____
_____	**MOMMA, TELL ME A STORY** (hardback)	**$12.95**	_____
_____	**MOMMA, TELL ME A STORY** (paperback)	**$ 6.95**	_____
_____	**FLICK THE HERO!** (hardback)	**$13.95**	_____
_____	**FLICK THE HERO!** (paperback)	**$ 7.95**	_____

SUBTOTAL ___ _____

POSTAGE ($1.50 1st book + .50 each add'l) + _____

S.C Residents only: add 5% sales tax + _____

TOTAL $ _____

Send check/ money order payable to: **WORRYWART PUBLISHING COMPANY**
337 WHITE BIRCH CIRCLE
COLUMBIA, S.C. 29223- 3228

SHIP TO: _____
_____
_____
_____